S0-CDL-268

Young People's

Stories of Truthfulness

Truthfulness is... being honest, even when it is hard.

Truthfulness is... sharing information that is important.

Truthfulness is... telling the whole truth, not just part of the truth.

Truthfulness is... stronger than lies.

Truthfulness is... known in the heart of the person who speaks it.

Compiled by
Henry and Melissa Billings

Young People's Press
San Diego

Editorial, design and production by
Book Production Systems, Inc.

Cover illustration by Gwen Connelly.

Published in the United States of America.

3 4 5 6 7 8 9 – 99 98 97 96

ISBN 1-885658-14-1

I Never Before Heard of Such a Thing (Zaire) .... page 2
illustrated by Susan Keeter

Truth and Falsehood (Greece) .... page 12
illustrated by Eldon C. Doty

The Truth (Syria) .... page 20
illustrated by Gwen Connelly

Acknowledgments .... page 30

I Never Before Heard of Such a Thing

This story comes from Zaire. It shows how a father and mother teach their young son to tell the truth. The word* Iteneinoso *means "I never before heard of such a thing."

A father and son went into the forest to hunt meat. They set traps to catch animals. The father set traps on the ground. He hoped to catch antelopes, wild pigs, and other animals. The son went up into the trees to set his traps. He hoped to catch monkeys, birds, and other tree animals.

That night the father said, “Son, go and check the traps we set. See if we have any animals in them.”

The son found a very large wild pig in one of the traps his father had set. The son killed it. He put it across his shoulder and took it back to his father.

“Father,” he said, “I found this wild pig in one of the traps in the tree where I had set them.”

“Is that true?” asked the father. “Is that really where you found the wild pig?”

“Yes,” said the son. “That is where I found it. Let us cut it up.”

“Very well,” said the father. “But I will need a special knife to cut up a wild pig like this. Go home and ask your mother to give you the knife which I call *Iteneinoso*.”

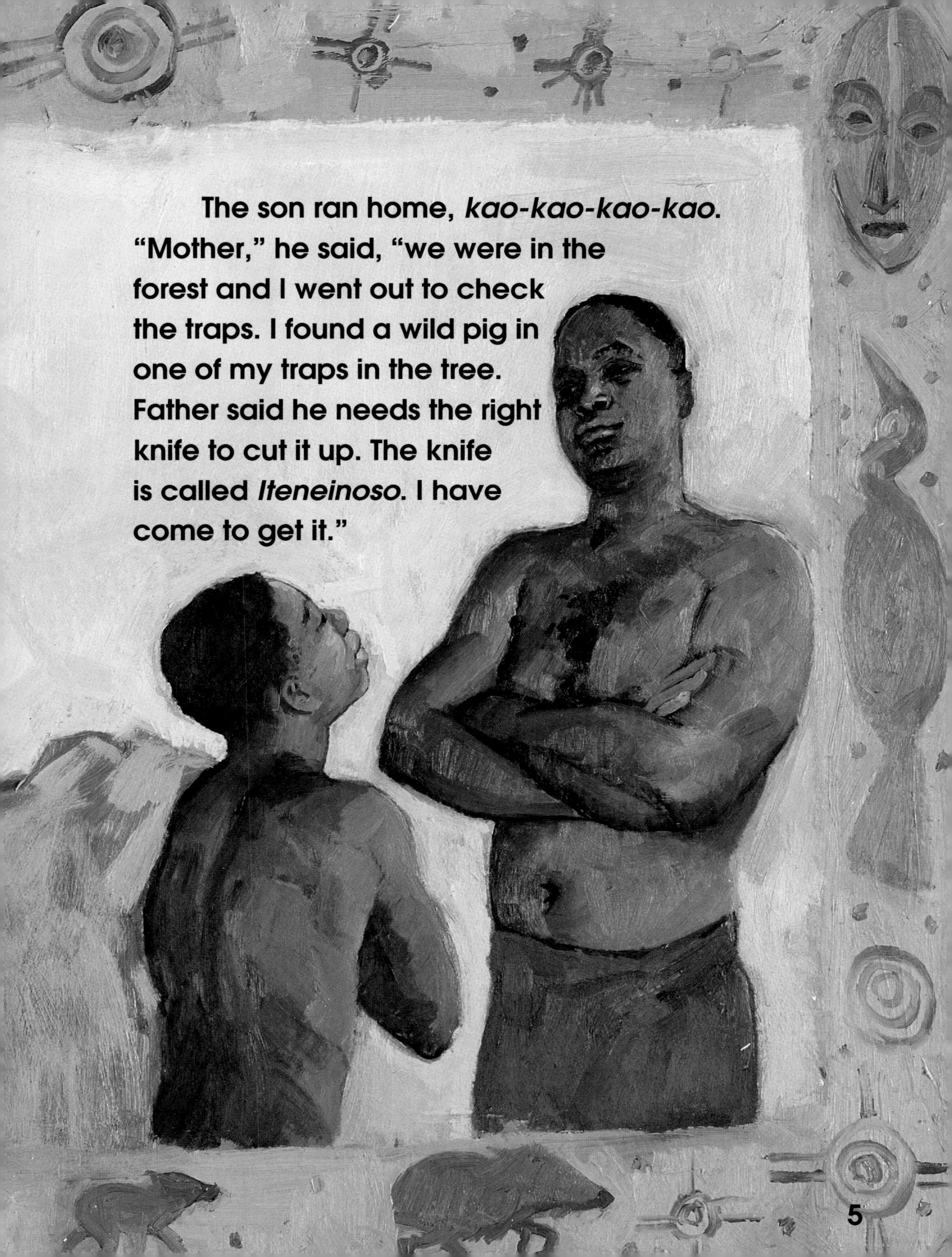

The son ran home, *kao-kao-kao-kao*. "Mother," he said, "we were in the forest and I went out to check the traps. I found a wild pig in one of my traps in the tree. Father said he needs the right knife to cut it up. The knife is called *Iteneinoso*. I have come to get it."

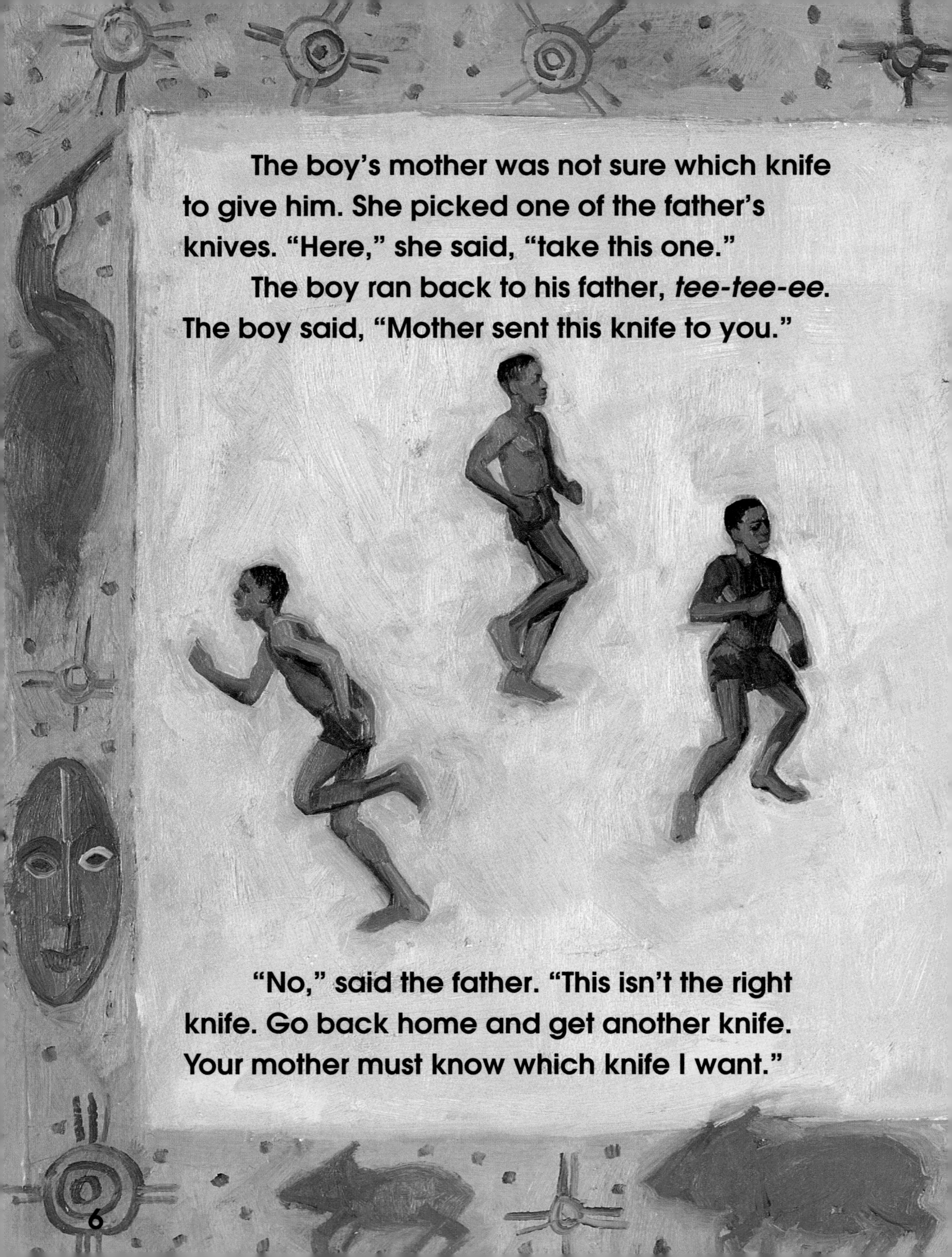

The boy's mother was not sure which knife to give him. She picked one of the father's knives. "Here," she said, "take this one."

The boy ran back to his father, *tee-tee-ee*. The boy said, "Mother sent this knife to you."

"No," said the father. "This isn't the right knife. Go back home and get another knife. Your mother must know which knife I want."

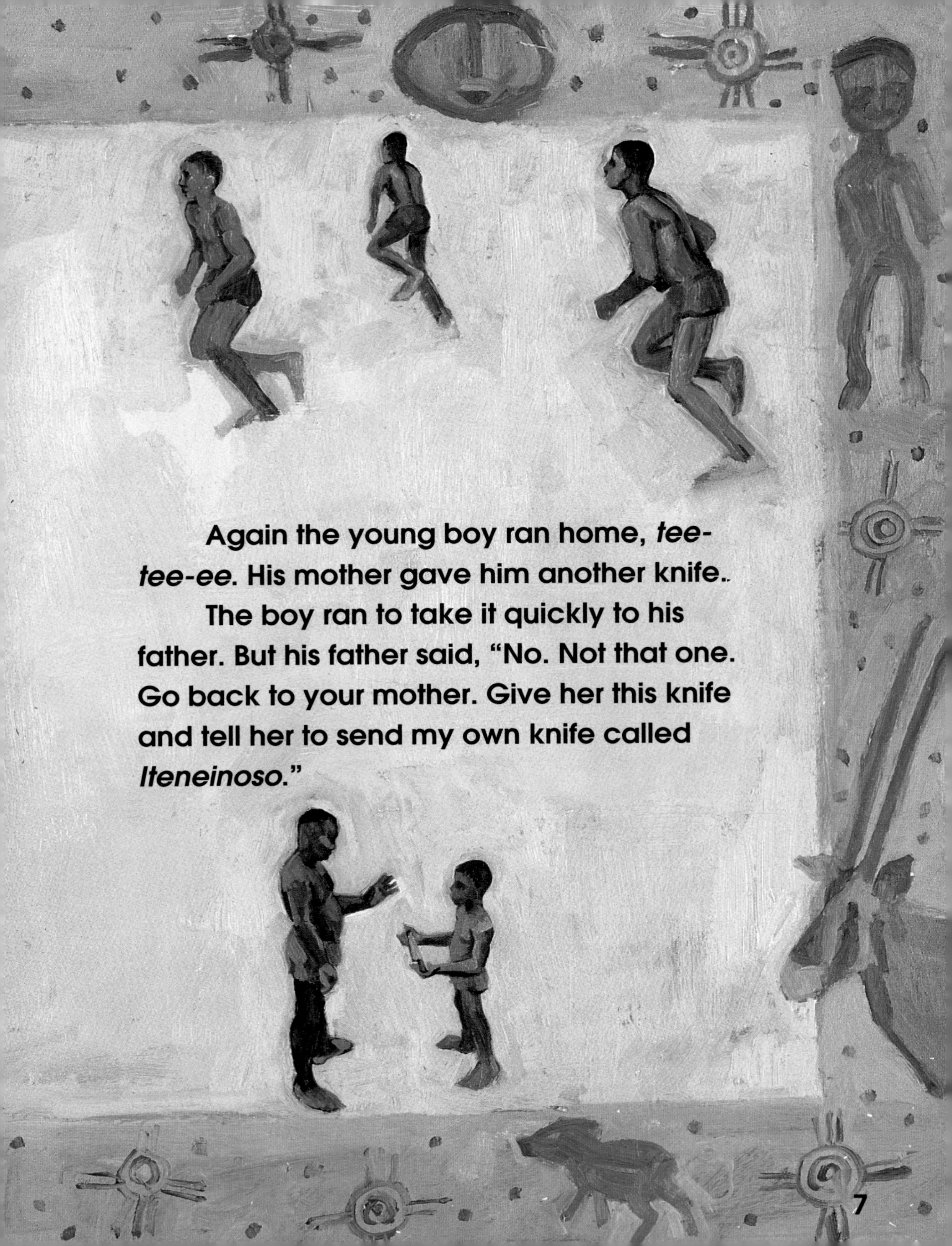

Again the young boy ran home, *tee-tee-ee*. His mother gave him another knife.

The boy ran to take it quickly to his father. But his father said, "No. Not that one. Go back to your mother. Give her this knife and tell her to send my own knife called *Iteneinoso*."

"Mother," cried the boy as he arrived home, "this isn't the knife that Father wants. He wants the one called *Iteneinoso*."

The mother sat down. She looked at the boy. Then she said, "My son! What am I to do? Tell me. Who killed the wild pig?"

"I did, Mother, with my knife."

"How did you do it?" she asked.

"With the trap I set in the trees," said the boy. "I killed it, and Father sent me for his special knife."

The mother laughed. "You say that the wild pig is yours because you found it in a trap in a tree. Pigs do not go up into trees. I have never before heard of such a thing. Are you sure this isn't your father's wild pig and not yours?"

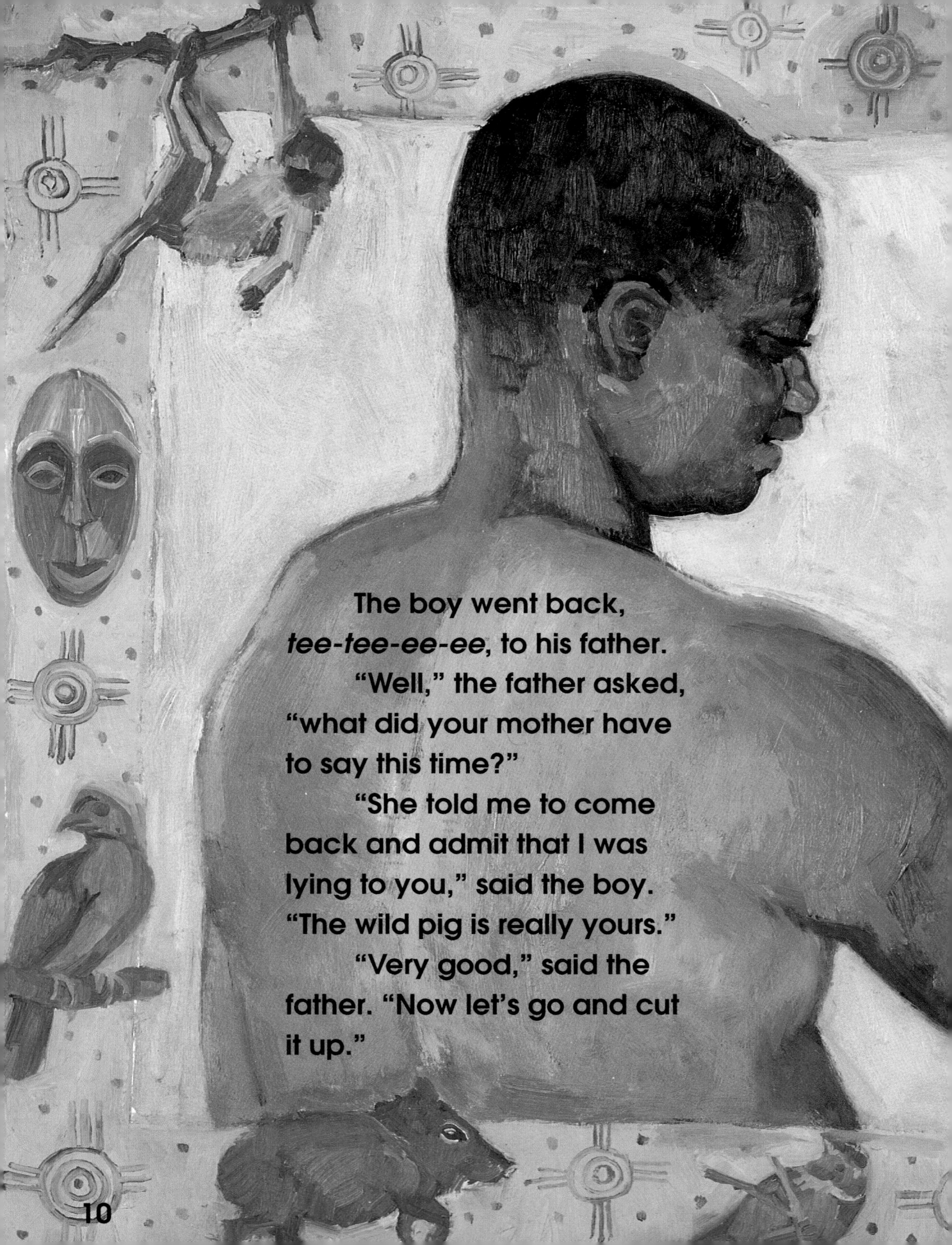

The boy went back, *tee-tee-ee-ee*, to his father.

"Well," the father asked, "what did your mother have to say this time?"

"She told me to come back and admit that I was lying to you," said the boy. "The wild pig is really yours."

"Very good," said the father. "Now let's go and cut it up."

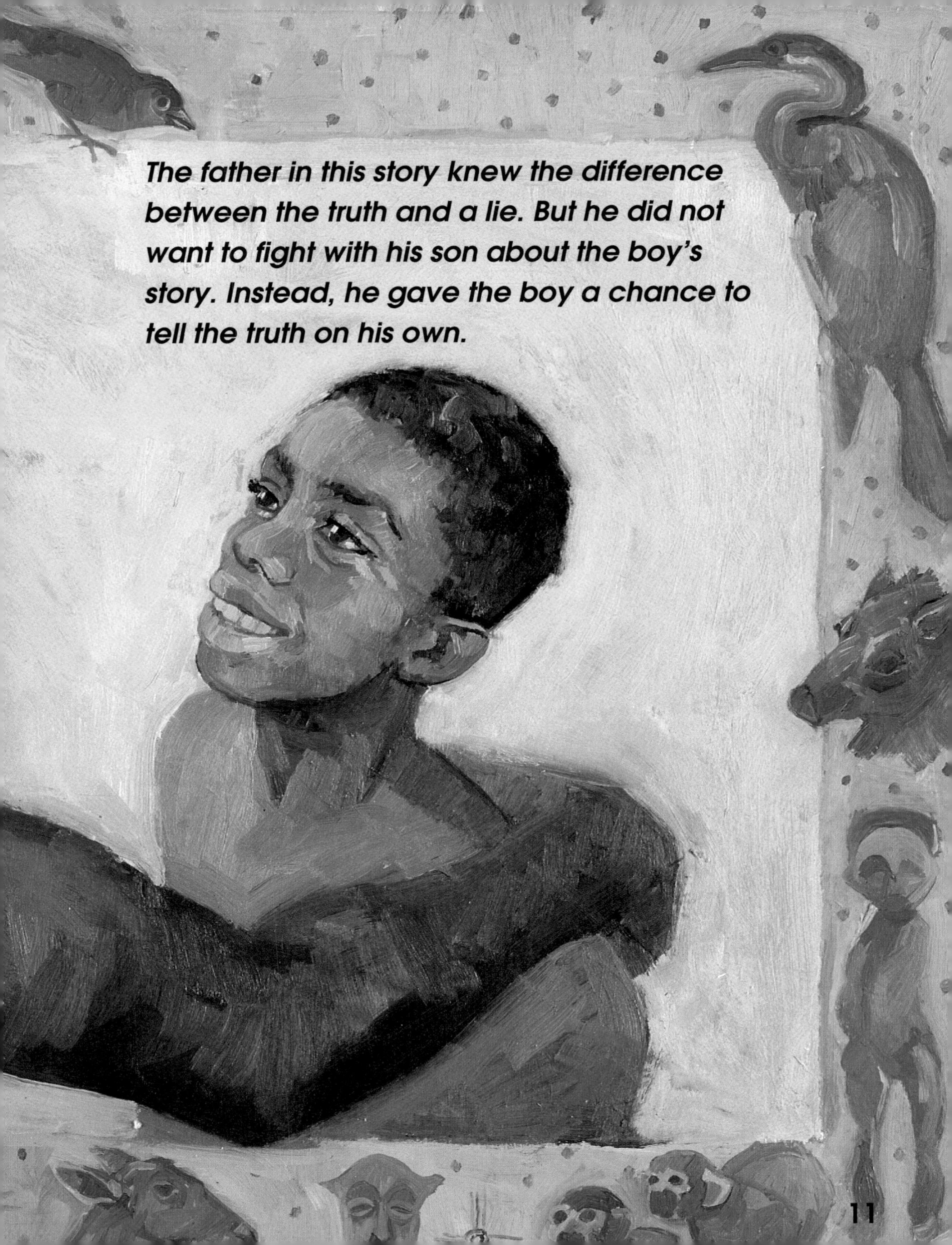

The father in this story knew the difference between the truth and a lie. But he did not want to fight with his son about the boy's story. Instead, he gave the boy a chance to tell the truth on his own.

This story comes from Greece. It shows that being truthful can be hard at times. In this case, telling a lie can help someone who is starving to get food. Read to find out if lying pays off.

Truth and Falsehood

Once, Truth and Falsehood met at a crossroads. After they had greeted each other, Falsehood asked Truth how things were going for him.

“Each year worse than the last,” said Truth sadly. “Not a bite has passed my lips for three days. Wherever I go, I get troubles—not only for myself, but for the few who love me still. It’s no way to live.”

“Well, you have only yourself to blame,” said Falsehood to him. “Come with me. You’ll see better days. You will dress in fine clothes like mine. You will eat plenty. I have only one rule: you must not challenge anything I say.”

Truth was so hungry he could barely stand up. So he decided, just this once, to go and eat with Falsehood. They set out together and soon came to a great city. Falsehood led Truth into the best hotel, which was full of people. They sat down and ordered the best food on the menu.

After they had eaten, Falsehood began to bang his fist on the table. The hotelkeeper herself came up to see what was wrong. She thought that Falsehood, who was dressed in fancy clothes, was a great nobleman.

"What is the matter?" she asked Falsehood.

"I gave money to the boy who sets the table," said Falsehood. "I told him to settle my bill and then bring me my change. I have been waiting a long time now. How much longer must I wait?"

The hotelkeeper called the boy over. The boy knew he had been given no money, and he said so. Then Falsehood pretended to grow angry. He began to shout.

"I would never have believed that such a fine hotel would rob the people who come here to eat! But I will bear it in mind the next time I am looking for a meal!" Falsehood threw money at the hotelkeeper. "There!" he said. "Bring me the change!"

The hotelkeeper feared that her hotel would get a bad name. So she refused to take the money. Instead, she gave Falsehood the change that he said he deserved. Then the hotelkeeper boxed the ears of the poor honest boy.

The boy began to cry. He continued to say that he had not been given any money. “No one believes me!” he sobbed. “Alas, where are you, unhappy Truth? Are you gone forever?”

“No, I am here,” said Truth through clenched teeth. “But I had not eaten for three days and I agreed not to speak during this meal. I am sorry, but I cannot help you now.”

When they got outside, Falsehood burst out laughing. “You see?” he said to Truth. “I know how to get what I want.”

“I would rather die of hunger,” said Truth, “than do the things you do.”

So Truth and Falsehood parted company forever.

This story shows that it is never wise to lie. Truth made a mistake when he agreed to keep his mouth shut for a free meal. He did not see his mistake right away. It took the honesty of the young boy to remind him. Because Truth knew the difference between right and wrong, he quickly got back on the right path. We need to be like Truth in this story. We all make mistakes. But if we remember right from wrong, we too can get back on the right path.

The Truth

This story comes from Syria. It tells about the truth that comes from the heart.

A king once ordered that anyone who told a lie would have to pay a large fine—five dinars, or gold coins, for each lie. When the members of the kingdom heard this order, they became afraid. They did not want to be caught telling a lie. They began to avoid each other.

The king wanted to know if his subjects were following his order. So one day he disguised himself and went to the marketplace. He soon came to the store of a rich merchant. He stopped in front of the door. The merchant invited him in and served him coffee. The two of them began to talk.

"How old are you?" the king asked.

"Twenty," said the merchant.

"What are you worth?"

"Seventy thousand."

"How many children do you have?"

"One."

When the king returned to the palace, he checked the records. Then he sent for the merchant. "How old did you say you were?" the king asked.

"Twenty," said the merchant.

"That will cost you five dinars."

"And how much are you worth?"

"Seventy thousand."

"That will be another five dinars. And how many sons do you have?"

"One," said the merchant.

"Pay another five dinars."

"First prove your case against me," said the merchant.

"You are an old man—sixty-five years old, according to the books. Yet you claim you are only twenty!"

"The years I enjoyed and in which I found happiness are but twenty—of the rest I know nothing," said the merchant.

"Then what about your riches? Your fortune is so large that it cannot be counted. Yet you say you are worth only seventy thousand."

"With those seventy thousand I built a mosque. That is my fortune—the money I gave to Allah and man."

"Well, you told me you have only one son. The records show you have six." The king then named the sons one by one.

"Five of those you have named have broken the commands of Allah. Only one, may Allah look kindly on him, is upright and good."

"You have spoken well, O truthful one," the king admitted. "No time is worth remembering but that which was passed in peace and happiness. No riches are worth counting but those spent for Allah and man. And no son is worth mentioning unless he is honest and good."

The truth in this story is not the truth found in numbers. Yes, in one sense it is "true" that the merchant had more money than he could count, was 65 years old, and had six sons. But in his heart, he saw a more important or "higher" truth. Once the king heard this "truth," he saw it too. He knew that the merchant had not told a lie.

Acknowledgments

Grateful acknowledgment is made for permission to reprint the following copyrighted material:

"The Rightful Owner," adapted for readability and retitled "I Never Before Heard of Such a Thing," from *"On Another Day . . ." : Tales Told Among the Nkundo of Zaire,* by Mabel H. Ross and Barbara K. Walker. (Hamden, CT: The Shoe String Press [an Archon Book], 1979), © Mabel H. Ross and Barbara K. Walker, used by permission of the authors, now holders of all rights.

"Truth and Falsehood" from FOLKTALES OF GREECE, edited by Georgios A. Megas, translated by Helen Colaclides. Copyright © 1970 University of Chicago. Adapted by permission of the University of Chicago Press.

"The Truth" from ARAB FOLKTALES by Inea Bushnaq. Copyright © 1986 by Inea Bushnaq. Adapted by permission of Pantheon Books, a division of Random House, Inc.